THIS WALKER BOOK BELONGS TO:

_____

_____

_____

First published 2000 by Walker Books Ltd
87 Vauxhall Walk, London SE11 5HJ

This edition published 2001

10 9 8 7 6 5

© 2000 A. E. T. Browne & Partners
Browne font © 2000 A. E. T. Browne & Partners

This book has been typeset in Browne; handlettering by Anthony Browne

Printed in Italy

British Library Cataloguing in Publication Data:
a catalogue record for this book
is available from the British Library

ISBN 0-7445-8240-7

www.walkerbooks.co.uk

This book is
dedicated to all
the great artists
who have inspired
me to paint

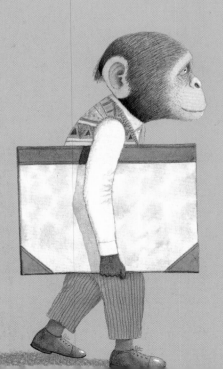

Look out for
their pictures at
the back of this book

WILLY'S PICTURES

Me   Millie   Buster Nose

Anthony Browne

WALKER BOOKS
AND SUBSIDIARIES
LONDON · BOSTON · SYDNEY · AUCKLAND

Willy likes painting and looking at pictures.
He knows that every picture tells a story…

THE BIRTHDAY SUIT

Quick, cover yourself up!

MY BEST EVER SANDCASTLE

I was so pleased with it, but I had an odd feeling
that the castle was trying to warn me of something.

LOTS AND LOTS AND LOTS OF DOTS

We gradually started to notice some
very strange things in the park.

THE KIND WOMEN

I had been getting a bit bored with painting all that grass.

EARLY MORNING DREAM

I'm just taking my dog for a walk. . .

MY BIRTHDAY

At first I thought it was great fun, but would they *ever* stop?

AT THE SWIMMING-POOL

Oh no, it's the wrong changing-room!

COMING TO LIFE

I was just finishing this painting when I heard
a small voice say, "Give us a hand."

THE MYSTERIOUS SMILE

Can *you* solve the mystery?

THE FRUITFUL FISHING TRIP

We hadn't caught anything all day and were on our
way home when we cast our net for the last time.

ROOM WITHOUT A VIEW

I had always hated looking out of that window,
so one morning I decided to do something about it.

MY NIGHTMARE

The dreadful invitation read, "You are cordially invited to attend the wedding ceremony of Millie and Buster Nose."

AN ODD DAY

As soon as we got there it seemed that Millie was in a hurry to go home. "I'm sorry," she said, "I must fly." And she was off!

LANDSCAPE WITH ONION

We followed it for miles before we finally hunted it down.

NEARLY A SELF-PORTRAIT

Some of my friends wanted to help.

THE HERO

I can dream, can't I?